Ann Hunter

This is a work of fiction. All the characters and events portrayed in this novel are fictitious, portrayed fictitiously, or align coincidentally to real persons and events.

Text copyright ©2014 Ann Hunter.

Stock cover photograph copyright ©2007-2014 Kayleigh Emerson. (http://kayleighemerson.deviantart.com/art/Red-Hen-393943802)

Graphic Designer: Andrew A. Gerschler.

Paragraph Break Designer: Willow Scott.

Interior Design: LibrisPro (www.librispro.com)

Published in 2014 by Afterglow Productions in association with P. Gerschler. All rights reserved. No part of this publication may be reproduced, stored in a retrieval system, or transmitted in any form or by any means, electronic, mechanical, photocopying, recording, or otherwise without written permission of the publisher.

A Piece of Sky by Ann Hunter.

ISBN-10: 0-9892034-1-7
ISBN-13: 978-0-9892034-1-8

OTHER TITLES BY ANN HUNTER

CROWNS OF THE TWELVE SERIES

The Subtle Beauty

Moonlight

Fallen

COMING SOON

Moredread

Blade of Woe

Ashes

North Oak

PRAISE FOR ANN HUNTER

With her gift for writing, Ann Hunter will sweep you away into a fairytale world that will steal your heart and fuel your imagination.

— The Tome Tender (Amazon top 500 reviewer)

Hunter blends fae and celtic mythos with modern-day fables in a seamless fashion. She has mastered the art of retelling fables…

— LV Adams
Ramblings & Musings of a Caffeine-Addicted Mind

She's the kind of writer who is so talented you think to yourself, "I wish I wrote like this."

—Amazon review

This is a writer to watch.

—Amazon review

CONTENTS

One
IN THE BEGINNING
1

Two
ALL WHO WANDER ARE NOT LOST
7

Three
THE ACORN
13

Four
A PIECE OF SKY
21

Five
CALL OF NATURE
34

Six
MOUNTAINS ABOVE
57

Seven
VALLEYS BELOW
73

Eight
A FAULT IN THE STARS
90

Nine
THE LAWS OF MAGIC
116

Ten
BAD SEED
126

Eleven
THE CHOSEN ONE
132

Twelve
WHAT THE CLUCK
138

Thirteen
CHICKEN LITTLE
150

To Blanchard, Reil, Woolley, and Rampton…
Because of your belief in my potential, you helped
me become a piece of sky.

Thank you.

Be the acorn...

IN THE BEGINNING

I

I was formed at the dawn of creation. When the darkness turned into light, the seas parted, and the first tree grew. The Father Tree, the god oak—I was part of him.

It happened so long ago, I cannot recall if I was the god oak, or the seed. All I remember is shooting up and out toward the heavens, and dangling like a tear on an eyelash. Waiting. I'm not sure for what.

Because I remained so wrapped up in the quandary of who I was, a considerable amount of time passed before I became aware of someone. He stood with his back to my trunk. He was cloaked in white with grand, transparent wings, wielding a sword licked by flame. As part of a tree, one might think I'd be frightened by fire, but I was curious.

Hello, I said.

An angular face peered over the wings with eyes as beautiful as the stars. His hair shared the complexion of the moon.

Unfortunately, he did not say hello back. Hanging around by myself was lonely. So I tried again the following night—or perhaps years passed. Time seemed to stand still where I lived.

Hello, I said.

I received a similar response as before. Not cold, but still wordless. Undeterred, I tried again some time later.

Hello! I said, louder. *Can you hear me?*

"Yes," he said without looking back. "But we should not speak to one another."

We should not… what? *Why?*

I would break one of the laws of the world if I told you.

But I'm lonely. Then wonder struck. How did his voice fill me without him speaking? *Who are you?*

His shoulders raised and lowered with a long breath. *I am Abaven, Captain of Queen Uonaidh's Guard. I have been stationed here to protect the Father Tree, The Tree of Life. I am of the Fae.* He finally faced me.

What's an Oon-nod? I asked. *Do I have one?*

His expression lightened, as though my questions amused him. I liked that.

Are you lonely too? I pressed. *I would like a friend.*

I am here to guard the world from you, not to make friends.

Why can't we be friends? A thought jarred me. *Wait. You said guard. Why do I need guarding? I am immovable.* I could not deny the panic rising in me. *What harm can I do?*

A smirk curled the corner of his mouth.

Why was he smiling? My panic grew. *Am I dangerous?*

I find it interesting you do not realize what you are.

Am I the tree, or the seed?

His silver eyebrow raised. *You really do not know what you are?*

I only know one truth: I wish to grow.

That is why I stand guard. I cannot allow you to do that. His brow creased like a wrinkle of bark. *Not now.*

But why?

Because of what you are capable of. Because you will shift the balance of the earth.

I trembled. *So I'm dangerous.*

I shrank when he said nothing. I didn't speak to him for a long time. How could I be dangerous? I was only a seed… or was I the tree? What made my desire forbidden?

Abaven?

He glanced to me from the corners of his eyes.

What makes me dangerous?

He remained silent, as though contemplating how to tell me.

Am I evil? I asked. The thought that I might be, rent me to my core.

You are the most powerful force on earth. His face tilted up. *You are beautiful and wonderful… but in the wrong hands, you would destroy the world.* He laid a hand on my trunk. His touch was warm and gentle, despite being strong enough to wield a flaming sword. I shivered. *Which is why you must be protected. It is for your own good.*

What happens if I escape this eden? Why are we the only ones here? I couldn't resist the urge to push against my shell. *I want to grow.*

He sighed. *The last souls to wander here were cast out for similar desires. I am here to ensure no one finds this tree again. The results would shift the balance irrevocably.*

Abaven, what is that behind you?

I watched him round on a hulking creature comprised of thick, twisted vines, with horns and hollows where eyes should be. The breaths it drew rattled between thorny ribs.

"Turn away while you still can," my Fae guardian growled.

The creature bellowed and stormed forward. Abaven's sword whooshed as it sliced the air, repelling the monster. The beast lunged again, smashing Abaven into my trunk. They grappled and threw each other, then charged and crashed again. Over and over, raging. Abaven fought valiantly, worthy of his station, but was knocked unconscious. I swung from the impact of their warring.

And then I tumbled through the ether. The god oak towered over me. I was definitely the seed.

Will someone please pick me up? I called. *I don't want to be alone. I need to grow.*

Vine-tangled fingers wrapped around me.

ALL WHO WANDER ARE NOT LOST

2

t was the sort of night that makes one want to hide beneath their bed covers…

KA-BOOM!

Thunder woke a little red hen who had been nesting peacefully in a small lean-to abutting Farmer's work shack. A flash of lightning illuminated a white hen beside her.

"Grania, did you hear that?" asked the red hen.

Grania stirred. "Go back to sleep, Rós. It's only thunder."

Rós turned her head in the direction

of a distant rumble. Lightning flashed again. She rustled her feathers, blinked, and begrudgingly nestled back down.

BOOM!

Rós leapt to her feet. "That was no thunder."

She stared at the other chickens who did not seem bothered by the storm, and wondered how they were sleeping through this. She took a hesitant step toward the edge of the lean-to.

Rumble, Rumble.

Black and purple clouds glowed around a shock of lightning. A hill in the distance brightened, capped by a circle of swaying trees. *I don't remember them being there before,* Rós thought. She glanced back to the other hens. "Grania," she whispered. "Grania, I'm going to find out what the noise is. Come with me."

"Rós, it is the middle of the night, and it is only thunder." Grania tucked her head beneath her wing groggily. "No one is awake but you. Now go to sleep."

Rós cocked her head from one side to the other. "It's not thunder." She stepped from the shelter of the lean-to, into a gust of wind. She blinked, staring at the hill in the distance. "There's something out there."

When the creature took me from the garden, I thought my plea to leave and grow had been answered. But as he held me between his viny, spindly, clawed fingers, I began to note the difference between him and Abaven.

Abaven's touch had been warm, like a ray of light. The creature's was dark and cold. I felt as though I'd been lessened somehow. Tainted. Covered in sludge.

Beneath Abaven's care, the tendrils within my shell pushed outward, but the creature made me retreat to my core. He stole me away to a grove on a hillside.

"I am Nurgal, Lord of Decay, and this…" He bore me toward the stars. "This is the answer to our problems. For too long man has pushed back against us, cutting us down, burning us, ruining our beautiful world for their own expansion. No more! I call upon you, Tree Folk of the Summer Isle, to stand against them."

The Tree Folks' leaves shivered against one another, like the sound of sheeting rain. They swayed in resistance. *It is wrong to harm others.*

Nurgal, who billowed out clouds of darkness around him, growled. "No. They wrong you. Turn against them before it is too late!"

The trees groaned and creaked. Nurgal roared like thunder, "I bring you life when you are faced with death, and you choose death. We can make the world green again with this golden seed. Join me!"

I pulsed in Nurgal's fingers. He stared at me as a flash of lightning framed his twisted horns, set atop the writhing roots and vines that formed his face and hollow, black eyes. The answer to his problems, the power to change the world, rested in me. In that moment I realized he didn't want to help me at all. The way he wished to use me was what Abaven had been protecting me from. My desire changed from wanting to grow to wanting to escape.

One of the trees bent close to Nurgal, and swept me hard from the monster's hand. I spiraled through the air, carried on a gust of wind, to the audible raging of Nurgal.

Rós moved quickly over the land between the farm and the hill by herself, for she did not want to get caught in the full force of the gale. Her curiosity's demand to be sated grew with every step she took. The closer she came to the group of strange trees on the hill, the more she awed. A swirling mass of purple clouds lingered over them. Lightning flashed out of the black, void-like center.

An ordinary hen would have cowered at the base of that hill. Instead, puzzled Rós staggered over the quaking ground, listened to the trees creaking and the rumbles above, and watched branches claw the sky as though of their own volition.

It was the acorn, tumbling through the stormy night, that ensured Rós would never be an ordinary chicken ever again.

THE ACORN

Rós's eyes opened in a half-lidded stupor. Her head ached. She waited for her vision to adjust to millions of blurred colors assaulting her. She couldn't make head or tails of it. Song birds chirped through bright light. She rose dizzily, but collapsed. *Where am I? What happened?*

Everything was out of focus. She gathered her feet beneath her again and staggered toward one shining object. A golden acorn lay upon a few gray stones, fuzzy with their own kind of halo. Rós pecked it. *Shiny.*

A sound scraped through her head, similar to when Farmer sharpened his axe. She winced. When she opened her eyes, the world came into focus… but not at all as she had seen it before. A mixed array of colors enveloped every living thing, putting off an essence of its own individual self. She blinked. Even the air swirled. The sky streaked shades of blue she never realized existed. Clouds became fascinating in all of their silver-edged, billowing whiteness. She stared at the acorn and remembered…

A dark and stormy night. The acorn rocketing from the center of the swirling vortex like a golden, shooting star. Then…

WHACK!

Rós gaped. A piece of sky had struck her.

But how could a piece of sky look like an acorn? Acorns grew on trees, not on clouds. It couldn't be an acorn. Not really. It had soared like a star, and stars came from the sky. It *must* be a piece of sky.

If she found her way home, she and Grania might be able to learn more about it together.

She cast her sight to the top of the hill, and she tried to get her bearings. The spot that the grove had occupied now lay barren. A wide patch of good, green earth remained. This only served to disorient Rós further. She turned her head around, her body following a moment later, not unlike when Dog chased his tail. Even in their beauty, the colors disoriented her. *I'm lost.*

Her gaze came to rest again on the piece of sky. She stepped to it and plucked it from the rocks. It seemed to pulse warmly in her beak. A fleeting temptation to try and swallow it riddled her, but she seated it neatly beneath her wings near the crook of her neck instead.

You'll be safe there, little sky.

She felt like Abaven. She was warm and soft, like light in the garden. And I could hear her thoughts. I saw my reflection in her golden eyes.

Little sky. I couldn't believe I was more than a seed. Could I be as bright and wonderful as the sky? I stared at the heavens. Sunlight warmed my core. It felt right.

Sky, I thought. *I'm a piece of sky!*

Trusting her gizzard, for it was all she had to go on, Rós found her way home late in the afternoon. Grania raced to her as soon as Rós reached the outskirts of the farm.

"Where have you been? Farmer has been looking all over for you, and I've been so worried."

Rós craned around briefly to make sure only Grania listened. "I went looking for the sound. I found trees shaking and creaking. They sounded angry. I believe they were the storm."

Grania preened the red hen, and discovered the acorn. "What is this?"

Rós peered over her wing. "That is a piece of the sky."

Grania tilted her head. "It looks like an acorn."

Rós ruffled her feathers, undoing Grania's grooming. "Trust me, Grania. It's a piece of sky. It fell from the sky and hit me in the head."

Grania pecked it. "It's an acorn."

Rós gaped. Her tongue undulated with an exasperated breath. "No. It's a piece of sky."

"Iiiiiiiiit's," Grania bawked, "an acorn."

Rós pecked Grania.

"Ow!" said the white hen.

"It didn't strike *you* in the head. I know

what I saw. Trust me, it's a piece of sky."

Grania shook out her feathers, then preened them smooth again. "But what does it *do?*"

"Clucks if I know." Rós blinked, realizing this was the first time seeing her friend with such colors about her. A circle of wavy berry blue, encased in a shade of lilac exactly like the flowers, hummed around the white hen. "But I see things now. The world is brighter. I think this piece of sky might be magic." She turned her head and nudged the little sky beneath her feathers again. "Perhaps," she said as she smoothed the feathers over, "it is a piece of the sun?" She paused with her beak against the shell. "It's warm."

"What do you mean, you 'see things now'?"

"Colors, Grania." Rós lifted her head and took in her surroundings with wide, wondrous eyes. "Colors everywhere." Her gaze settled on her friend. "Maybe that is its purpose. It is magic, and it makes you see colors."

Grania cocked her head. "Whaaaat?"

Rós plucked the piece of sky from her back and snapped her head, flinging the golden thing at Grania. It caught her between the eyes. Grania toppled over.

"Oh my eggs, what did you do that for?" Grania's colors dimmed from blue to grayish green for a moment.

Rós trotted to her side, and retrieved the piece of sky. "Do you see colors now?"

Grania glared at her. "I'm seeing red."

The piece of sky dangled by its stem from Rós's beak. She tried not to feel too bad about the misjudgment, and placed the little sky on her back.

Grania found her unsteady feet and shook herself off. "It's not magic. It doesn't make you see colors. It's an acorn."

"I think we should get another opinion." Rós huffed. "My world has changed. I wish you would believe me."

Grania preened the back of her friend's head. "I believe you. I believe you were hit in the head with an acorn."

"Let us ask Dog."

"Why him? Won't he tell Farmer?"

"Are you concerned I might be right?" Rós's chest swelled. "Dog is honest, and he guards the farm. If this piece of sky is magic, we need to know."

"I bet you three eggs Dog won't know what to do with your acorn."

"It's a piece of sky," Rós said flatly.

"Three eggs."

The little red hen shook out her feathers. "Fine."

A PIECE OF SKY

ós and Grania stood several yards off from Dog who barked excitedly. "Chicken. Chicken… Chicken, chicken. Chicken!"

"Are you sure this is a good idea?" Grania asked.

Rós noted the enthusiastic shades of sunset pink and violet bubbling around Dog. They spiked when he barked.

He was a shaggy thing, half the size of the sheep, black and white like Cow, and as long and lean as a thread of lightning; built to move fast. He stayed tied near the end of Farmer's longhouse on the days they did not go into the highlands to herd. Dog had a terrible habit of neurotically circling the chickens and holding them captive whenever he was off the stake.

The piece of sky dangled by its stem from Rós's beak and she turned her head to one side. She became fairly certain the sheepdog would not harm them after his exuberant colors calmed to a barely contained line. Her head bobbed with each step toward him.

He sat on his haunches, wagging his tail and panting. His eyes fixed on the little sky, and one ear cocked. "Is that a treat? Did you bring me a treat?"

Rós placed the piece of sky before him. He sniffed it and shook his head. "It's not a bone."

Grania stepped beside Rós. "It's an acorn."

Rós glared at her, then looked back to Dog. "This piece of sky came out of the storm last night and hit me in the head.

Might you know anything about it?"

"Why would he know anything about it?" Grania bawked beneath her breath, her colors shifting to a stormier shade of blue.

Dog sniffed the piece of sky again and gave it a lick. His tail thumped the ground. "The sky you say? That was quite the gale last night."

"Yes it was," Rós concurred.

Grania rolled her eyes.

Dog nudged the piece of sky back to Rós with his nose. "Did you notice anything unusual?"

She seated the acorn in the safe spot on her back. "A grove of trees swayed on the hillside. They had never been there before, so I went to see about them. Purple clouds circled above the grove. The darkness at its center spat out the piece of sky."

Dog laid down and rested his chin on his paws. "Trees you say? Do you think they were E.N.T.s?"

"What's an E.N.T.?" Grania asked.

Dog's eyes moved to her. Rós rather thought they looked like two crescent moons, darkened by the starry night sky. He snuffed. "Evil Neurotic Trees."

"How can a tree be evil?" asked Grania.

Dog moistening his nose with his tongue. "They claw the sky." He whined. "They rip, they scrape, their leaves whisper in the wind. They even groan."

"That doesn't make them evil," Grania argued.

"Who's to say they did not cause the hole in the sky, and throw the piece at her?"

Rós puffed out her chest, and tilted her head to her friend. "See, Grania?"

Dog snuffed again. "Then again, it could be just an acorn."

Grania clucked to Rós. "You owe me three eggs."

Dog lifted his head and panted. "I'm not certain. You should definitely take this up with The Mare. A little piece of sky is awfully suspicious."

Rós trotted right up to him to offer her gratitude the way she had seen Farmer do. "Who's a good boy!"

Dog bowed on his front paws, tail wagging, and yipped. His colors went hyper-vivid. "Is it me? Oh, it's me, isn't it!" He rolled on to his back. "Rub my belly?"

Rós hopped up on his rib cage and scratched and pecked playfully.

"A little to the…" he started to say. His foot flapped in the air. "Oh, bones, that's the spot!"

Rós hopped off a moment later. "I'll bring you a treat as soon as I can, Dog."

He rolled back over, a smile on his face. His tail thumped the ground. "Please and thank you."

The little red hen returned to Grania after ensuring the piece of sky remained safe on her back. Grania was still stormy blue, and none too amused about the whole situation. "For the next three days, you owe me one of your eggs to give to Farmer," said the white hen.

"Not yet, Grania. Not until we visit The Mare. You heard Dog. This is bigger than we anticipated. If E.N.T.s are involved…"

Grania's feathers ruffled. "This nonsense is going to stop, Rós. It's only an acorn."

Rós trotted off in the direction of the pastures. "Wait and see, Grania. The Mare is old and wise, or she would not be The Mare of the entire farm."

They found The Mare on the greenest pasture, far back from the rest of the animals. It was a place of honor, for The Mare had spent her entire life working hard for Farmer.

She was gray and flea-bitten with a patch of red hairs running across her broad shoulder, and down to her knee.

Despite being well-fed and kept on the best pasture, her bones and ribs jutted out due to her advanced age. Farmer loved her to bits and kept her well groomed, but you wouldn't know with how threadbare her mane was.

"Forgive me, Your Honor," Rós clucked. "We don't mean to be a bother, but I was wondering if you could settle a matter for us."

The Mare's tail swished. "It's no trouble. Come closer."

Rós approached, admiring the way the horse glowed with an energy of soft sun-golds and cloud-silver.

The hen stared at her own reflection in the old mare's dark eyes. She hoped she would see the colors that surrounded herself, but alas, she did not. Was it because the gray horse did not see them?

The Mare's lower lip hung as Rós presented her with the bit of sky. The Mare whuffed and sniffed it.

"It's a piece of sky," Rós informed her. She glanced to Grania.

Three eggs, the white hen mouthed.

"Tell me how you found it," The Mare nickered.

"Well, Your Honor," Rós said, "we met with Dog first, and he mentioned E.N.T.s may be involved. He thinks they ripped it from the sky during the storm last night."

"I don't believe that was an ordinary storm," said The Mare. "I can't help wondering if something larger isn't at work. I hope the heavens are not about to come crashing down."

"It's an acorn," Grania grumbled.

The Mare's eyes bored through her. "I've yet to see an acorn like this. Sometimes the biggest forces can take the smallest form."

Grania's slowly-widening eyes shifted

to Rós who intently focused on The Mare.

The little red hen spoke humbly. "If I may say so, Your Honor, I believe this piece of sky holds such power. I viewed the world in a whole new way when it struck me. So many colors I never knew about sprang to life, as though another world exists around every living being. We cannot see it, save for our eyes being opened by a little piece of sky."

The Mare whickered. "What you have told me goes beyond my knowledge. I wish I could help you, but the best I can offer is to counsel you to seek the kelpie in the lake near the mountains. I believe man calls the place Lake Lomond."

Grania tilted her head to Rós. "Do you know how far that is?" she whispered.

Rós settled the piece of sky in its safe place on her back. "No," she murmured. "But I'm sure we can find it."

The Mare stepped closer to the two

hens and nuzzled them. "I wish you the best on your journey. Many perils will be on the way. Take care, little ones." She returned to grazing, turning her back to the hens.

Rós headed toward hazy mountains so far away they appeared as shadow and mist.

Grania blinked, trotting after her. "Where are you going?"

"You heard The Mare. We need to find the kelpie of Lake Lomond."

"But… that means leaving the farm. Rós, we can't leave the farm. Farmer needs us to lay eggs."

"I can't sit around laying eggs all day when E.N.T.s are ripping the sky apart." She paused long enough for her friend to catch up. The white hen's colors gained a touch of nervous red. "Grania, don't you ever wonder what's beyond the hills around our farm? Don't you ever wonder if there's *more* to life than laying eggs?"

Grania ruffled her feathers. "Rós, what are you saying?"

Rós stepped closer and preened Grania's feathers smooth, willing the colors to calm. "Come with me. You're my best friend. I wouldn't want to make this journey with anyone else."

Grania backed away. "I... I'm not sure I can."

Rós adjusted the little sky on her back. "Grania, for once in your life, don't be such a chicken. Take a leap of faith. Come with me."

"Those mountains are so far away," said Grania, her voice fraught with worry.

"We can make it. We can do this together. Come with me!"

Grania glanced over her shoulder, back to the farm. "We're safe here. We have food, and friends, and Farmer's protection. Life is perfect. Why would we want to leave?"

"Grania, the sky is falling! How can

you sit by and let it happen? We'll find food. We'll be together."

"But what if it's nothing? What if your piece of sky is only an acorn, and this is all getting bawked out of proportion? What if this—this *quest* you want to go on—is one big rotten egg?"

Rós looked to the mountains far beyond, then over her shoulder to the little sky, so warm and shiny against her russet feathers. Her eyes found Grania. "But what if it's not? The Mare said the largest forces can come in the smallest of sizes. I know this piece of sky looks like an acorn, but there has to be more." She scanned the horizon and took a step forward. "And I'm going to find out."

"Rós," Grania clucked. "Be reasonable. Think this through. Who knows what danger is out there?" She took a glimpse of the farm once more. The constant shift of her colors gave away how torn she was. "What do we know about this kelpie? What *is* a kelpie?"

Rós egged her on. "Did you say three eggs or four?"

Grania huffed. "I don't want to leave home, but I can't let you go alone."

"You can." Rós bawked, "I love you, but you have to make this decision on your own. I don't know what's out there… but I do know I can face it with you by my side."

CALL OF NATURE

"I'm so glad you decided to come with me, Grania."

"How long do you think this will take?" sighed Grania. "Because I... I mean *Farmer* will be wanting those extra eggs."

Rós shifted her wings in a shrug-like manner. "Clucks if I know." She glanced to her friend. "Does it matter as long as we have one another?"

Grania bawked softly. A smattering of buttercup yellow punctuated her blue.

"I'm sure we'll make it by twilight." Rós did not like lying, but part of her wanted to believe it, even though the mountains on the horizon remained hazy silhouettes against the sky. Her comment eased Grania's colors back to berry blue with that pretty lilac Rós liked.

Sometimes we have to stretch the truth to survive really difficult hardships. We tell ourselves whatever we have to in order to endure. Rós did this with her friend, and I believe both of them knew it at the time.

They would tell one another that the journey would be over as soon as they found the kelpie. It wouldn't take long to get there. But do you know how far a chicken walks in a day?

About as far as Nurgal threw me.

I think as time wore on, people began to say that such and such was an acorn's throw from someplace else. Rós and her friend started it. Though Rós would never call me just an acorn.

I remember dusk, and the white hen looking over her shoulder.

"It's not too late, you know."

"Too late for what?" Rós often walked ahead of her. Doing so gave me a good view.

"To go home," Grania said. "We can go back."

"How far do you think it is?"

"About as far as I can throw that acorn."

I think Rós must have felt me shiver, for she paused and readjusted me on her back. *Don't worry, little sky, you're not going anywhere.*

She squinted at her friend. "We're not going back, Grania. Unless you want me to keep the eggs."

The white hen gawked at the trees around us, and the cool, dimming horizon. "It's getting dark." She looked at Rós. "I don't like being out in the open like this."

"We'll be alright. We just need to stay together. Four eggs, now, remember?"

"You said we would be there by nightfall."

"I think you knew when I told you that it wasn't true. Remember the time we told ourselves we wouldn't steal treats from Pig's trough anymore? We both knew, deep down inside, that it wasn't true, because sometimes we tell ourselves things to get by. You're here now. Stay with me."

Grania sighed. "Can we rest here? I'm tired."

Rós's eyes turned skyward and filled with starlight. "Here is perfect."

The three of us bedded down right there. The two hens nestled close together to keep each other warm. Rós tucked me beneath her beak with her head under her wing. I couldn't get over how warm she felt.

The following morning we were up and off with the rising of the sun. A spot of light forever glinting off the path, always just out of reach, kept Rós engaged. *Shiny!* was her constant thought, penetrating her mind to a primal depth.

"It's a shiny new day," she said cheerily.

Grania grumbled and trudged along. "I'm hungry."

"So eat. I'll wait." Rós paused in the middle of the path.

Grania took a deep breath. "Farmer isn't here to feed us."

"Oh, don't be silly, Grania. You know how to rustle up some grubs."

The white hen clucked. "I want mash."

"That old slop?" Rós opened her beak slightly, showing her tongue. "We're wild chickens now." She pecked at an insect crossing her path, her words punctuated by a full mouth. "Om-nom." The bug popped in her mouth, emitting a delicious crunchy, smacking sound from her beak.

"Eat up."

Grania rolled her eyes.

"Do not complain about being hungry when we are surrounded by food," Rós admonished. "There's no excuse out here. We want for nothing."

"I want Farmer," Grania clucked beneath her breath.

Rós skittered up the path. "I want to get to the lake."

I noted the white hen had no argument for that. She followed behind for some time, but as the sun began to set, she slowed.

"I'm tired. My wing hurts."

"Oh, that's not good. Which wing?"

Grania dragged her feet. "My beak hurts and my legs are tired."

The red hen glanced over her shoulder. Grania gazed back, lackluster with gray. The bald sky faded from blue to blossom pink beneath a haze of orange behind her. "We can bed down for the night,"

Rós said. "I think we made good progress today."

"The mountains seem no closer than when we left."

Rós found a soft spot in some grass near the side of the trail. She preened her feathers. "They will soon enough, I'm sure of it."

Her friend sighed and toddled over, taking up a spot beside her.

As they nestled into sleep, I settled into my own thoughts. Nothing in particular, really. Have you ever lain awake at night and allowed your mind to roam while you waited for the rest of yourself to ease into slumber? It was that sort of feeling. I thought about the god oak and Abaven, and how different and alive the world outside of the garden was.

For the first time, I was fully aware of the world. A vast one with a touch of the terrifying. Since leaving the garden, I had been flung through a storm, licked, snorted on, and used as a weapon against another chicken. (That last bit hit me right in my Oon-nod.)

There were so many new things to take in. With a rise of panic, it became clear how overwhelming it all could be. I took in our surroundings and tried to calm myself.

Tree…

I looked to another one. *Tree…*

One more. *Another tree…*

The sound of crickets made me glad I wasn't the only one still awake. Their music helped soothe me. I still couldn't get over how soft the little red hen was. I counted her with the trees. *Chicken…*

A brief lull. *Rocks…*

Something moved in the darkness of the woods. I startled to full alertness. *Not a tree.* We were being spied on.

A twig snapped. Leaves on the ground rustled. I trembled at the sound of breathing filling the empty space.

Panic grew in me, and if it had not been so paralyzing I would have cried out to warn the hens. *I wish you would wake up!*

Rós stirred. I could tell her brain remained fuzzy, until she finally saw what I did, and nudged her friend. The white hen's eyes opened.

"Grania, I think we should go."

Grania raised her head and locked on to what Rós and I saw: two eyes illuminated by the moon staring back at us, and ever so subtly the glare of teeth.

Something deeper within me, something silent and intangible willed, *Run!*

In a tangle of feathers and claws, the hens bolted. Everything was a jumble from there.

"This way," one squabbled.

The sound of their feet picking over the pebbles and dirt of the path was frantic.

Scrape... grind... Whoosh!

…like the fall of hail.

"Don't look back," cackled the other.

Grania glanced over her shoulder. "It's a fox!"

He panted behind them, yipping with excitement.

We raced through the forest, over knolls and around stones. Rós's breath rushed like the summer wind, coming in short, gray puffs on the cold spring air. "Faster."

We bolted into a ravine. "I don't know if I can," Grania called back.

Rós darted to the right just as the fox lunged at their feet. The red hen careened up a narrow path. "Follow me Grania!" she panted. She raced ahead until she skittered to a stop where the ground dropped straight off, and soon realized her friend was nowhere to be seen.

"Grania?" She peered over the edge. The moon shone off of a large body of water. She retraced her steps. "Grania!"

Grania screeched. Rós darted in the direction of the voice. "I'm coming Grania!" She bolted so hard and fast, the piece of sky nearly came unseated from the spot on her back. She caught it just in time, and shrugged it back into place. After a short rustle through the grass, she stopped near a huge boulder overlooking the ravine. She had taken the high ground.

Grania raced down the gap below with the fox in mad pursuit. "Rós, help me," she cried.

Rós sprinted along the edge of the cliff. Even in the darkness their colors were visible. The fox circled Grania and glowed greedy red like the wattle of a rooster. "Tell a riddle," Rós hollered.

"What?"

"A riddle. Tell him a riddle."

"Why would I do that?"

"Trust me!" Rós begged. Her eyes scoured the layout of the ravine, and came to rest on the boulder beside her. A zing of inspiration struck her mind. She took off toward the trees and picked up a fallen branch, dragging it to the boulder.

Grania stood, horror-stricken, before the fox. He stalked ever closer.

"Why… did the… chicken…." She shuddered. "Rós I can't do this."

Rós forced the branch under the boulder. "You have to."

Grania's bawk rippled over the walls of the ravine. "Why did the chicken cross the path?"

The fox's ears perked. He stood stock still as though a simple riddle entranced him.

"She thought it was an egg-cellent idea."

"Another, Grania," Rós called, grunting as she worked the branch deep beneath the boulder. "Tell him another."

The white hen's voice got a little braver. "What do you get when a pig bumps into a chicken?"

The fox growled.

"Ham and eggs," Grania cackled.

Rós ran to the cliff's edge and gathered a stone to roll beneath the branch. She eased it under, then hopped on the branch, and bounced up and down. The boulder inched forward.

"My turn," said the fox. "Why did the fox chase the chicken?"

The branch Rós bounced on creaked and cracked with effort.

Grania's voice thickened with panic. "I refuse to answer that. No, no. Stay where you are. Rós!"

The boulder lurched over the edge. The fox let out a squeal, followed then by silence.

Rós dropped down onto the boulder and shook out her feathers. She blinked as if nothing had happened. "Look. There's the lake!" She motioned toward the still water nearby.

Grania breathed hard. "There's a rock."

Rós looked down. "That is a big rock."

"I never knew foxes liked riddles so much."

"It's their weakness." Rós shrugged. "Do you think you've ever laid an egg this big?" She hunkered down, wiggling her tail feathers, as though doing so would change the boulder into an egg.

The white hen preened herself, then backed away slowly. "You do realize that if the lake is over there, you've blocked the path."

Rós cast her gaze to the water. "Hmm. That is a problem."

"You go on ahead. I can wait here. I think I'll be alright. I can't imagine it will take you long."

Rós jumped down beside her friend without a second thought. "No. We do this together or not at all. We'll find another way around. Come on!"

How would you describe dreaming to someone who had never dreamed before?

I thought I had been with the little red hen a moment ago, but the world faded around me. The darkness was heavy, like the oppressive heat of summer. It was the sensation of falling from the god oak all over again, only it didn't end until Nurgal's fingers wrapped around me.

Vines creaked with his tightening grip, their slippery coating oozing over my shell. I was aware of his steady breathing, of the rattle of air between the vegetative elements that composed him. He walked with a quiet growl.

When he opened his hand, I saw Abaven laying unconscious at the base of the Father Tree, his silver hair matted with blood. Nurgal pinned me between his own finger and thumb, and I swear I heard his thoughts. *Little good it did you, guarding that tree.*

In an instant I plunged into the soil and barreled between the roots of the god oak. A dark, irresistible force overtook me. Green shoots rushed from my core, clawing at the roots of the tree and choking it to death.

No, I thought. *No, I don't want to destroy!*

But I couldn't stop. Wouldn't stop. Like a great force was at work on me bigger than I could understand.

Within moments, I tangled the god oak with my own vines. I was the antilife. The destroyer of worlds. The Father Tree writhed, fighting against me, but I was stronger.

Through the canopy, I watched stars race and fall across the sky. No longer like jewels in an untouched cavern, but a swirl of mass chaos streaking through the night.

The large, above-ground roots of the Father Tree tangled with my own. Some of my vines separated from the trunk and wrapped around Abaven. I bore him toward the heavens against my will. With every attempt to release him, I grew tighter and tighter, like the serpent that cast out man. Nurgal's vice-like influence overpowered my resistance. A dread filled me. My vines snapped the Fae guard in half as though he had not been more than a brittle twig.

I grieved.

And yet I still could not stop myself.

Nurgal's laugh grew louder, unnerving. I reached across the whole of the garden, squelching out everything in my path, for I did not possess the strength to resist the darkness on my own. What had once been beautiful and sacred now lay waste. And it didn't stop at the outskirts.

A PIECE OF SKY

My desire to grow was bigger than I was. Alone, I wasn't strong enough to stop it. Once out of the garden, it only grew wilder.

The earth went poison-green, and black, and purple, in a wake of verdant destruction. All that cropped up through time, all that was good... destroyed. Because of me.

Because I was the most powerful force on earth.

"Rós? What's that around your neck?"

I woke groggily and felt the red hen look down.

"I think..." Rós turned her head. "I think it's Little Sky."

"Little Sky?" the voice of the white hen posed.

"Yes, that's what I've decided to name it."

"When?"

"Just now," Rós pipped.

"It's choking you."

I suddenly realized that long, green tendrils had grown out from me, and I wrapped around the little red hen's neck. What I had seen frightened me and made me cling for dear life. I didn't know fear could make me grow like that. It had never happened before.

What do I do? I panicked, trying to pull the stems back in. I shook with effort. Air moved between the feathers and the tendrils smacked my shell awkwardly, first one side then the other.

Pop! Pop!

They disappeared within. I wish I could vanish completely.

The last thing I expected was for Rós to press her beak to me gently, as though it hadn't bothered her. "Look, Grania," she said quietly, "it's alive."

The noise I heard come out of the white hen did nothing for my self-esteem. Her shiver made me feel worse, like I was something to be feared.

Rós blinked. Sunlight peeked over the tree tops. "We better get moving. I think we'll make it to Lomond today."

By midday, they came to a large, still stream across from a hillside—too wide to hop across, too deep to wade through.

"How are we going to get to the other side?" Grania asked.

Rós scanned up and down the stagnant water. "Umm…" Her eyes fixated. "How about that giant tree that's laying around not doing anything?"

Grania followed her gaze to an ancient, moss-ridden brown trunk reaching across the banks. Mushrooms grew out the side, and the bottom littered the water with rotting bark. "You're not serious."

Rós circled to the front of the white hen. "Don't tell me you're a bigger chicken than the sheep."

Grania lifted her head indignantly. "I am not a dumb sheep."

The red hen chortled. "Baaaah!"

Grania's gaze settled firmly on Rós. "Stop it."

Rós flapped her wings. "Baaaah, baaaah!"

"Rós…"

The red hen danced around, singing. "Baaah, baah, Grania sheep, have you any wool?"

Grania's eyes narrowed. "You owe me five eggs."

Rós sobered up. "That's the spirit!" She picked her way over to the trunk and clambered on top, then glanced behind. Grania pecked at the roots that surged out like rays of sun.

"Are you sure this is safe?"

Rós was already halfway across. "Not at all!"

Grania clawed her way up and shivered.

The little red hen began to sing:

Down in the meadow
Where the bugs run deep
Chickens love to play and leap.

She hopped down on the far bank with the last word.

"Rós what are you doing?" Grania asked dryly.

"Singing. It helps. Try it."

Grania was halfway across the log now. She edged her foot out before her. Reeds reached toward her from the green water below.

I hate this log,
Above the bog...

Rós cocked her head to one side. "Do you hear that frog?"

A fat, bumpy bullfrog blinked at them. **"Brooog,"** he croaked. **"Brooog. Brooog."**

He dived into the water with a loud kerplunk.

Grania finally joined her friend on the safety of land. Rós smoothed the white hen's feathers. "Well done. You are definitely not a sheep."

The nightmare I'd had that morning was enough to make me wish to never dream again. I forced myself to stay awake. I tried so hard. But the constant motion of the red hen's waddle tempted me back again. I missed Abaven.

MOUNTAINS ABOVE
6

"*Where is it?*" Nurgal boomed.

In a hazy state, I saw rubble skitter down the walls of the cave Nurgal paced within. My vision came in cloudy patches, fuzzy on the outside. I had a sense of the Mountains of Tór that formed a curtain across the shores of the Shining Sea. A brief, dreamy glimpse revealed darkness cascading over their soaring, snow-blanketed peaks.

Hands bound, and upon his knees, was Abaven. To see him alive brought me boundless relief. I watched him draw an uneven breath, and taste a spot of blood on his swollen, broken lip. "The fact that you lost it tells me it does not wish to be yours."

Nurgal stooped to his eye level. "Tell me how to find it."

Abaven spit in his face. Nurgal bellowed and slammed him to the ground, ripping off the captain's wings.

The Fae guardian writhed, face contorted, and gasped. "You will… never find it."

Nurgal kicked him in the ribs. *"Tell me!"*

Abaven rolled on to his back, groaning, then lay in silence. He began to laugh.

Nurgal's shoulders heaved. "Why are you laughing?"

Abaven's laugh grew louder.

"Stop laughing!" Nurgal demanded.

"It's funny, isn't it," rasped the Fae guard, "that the one thing you seek refuses to seek you. It's lost to you, Nurgal. You've been outsmarted by… an… *acorn*. Your thievery was in vain."

"It's not an acorn!" The Lord of Decay backfisted him. Nurgal's breath was erratic. "It's so much more."

Abaven spit out a tooth, coughing. "You'll never find it, 'less it wishes to be found. It *used* you."

Nurgal growled.

Abaven continued. "It used you to escape. The acorn has been under my watch for centuries. I've learned a thing or two. You've taken and unleashed something you don't understand, and now it's only a matter of time."

He rose on his knees slowly, head bent. "The acorn has as much power to destroy as it does to give life. It is the most ancient and sacred force in the whole of creation."

My sight intertwined with Abaven's, and our gaze met the hollows in Nurgal's face with fierceness. "If there were any faculty higher than The Fae, I would pray to them that whomever the acorn has chosen is far more powerful than the Lord of Decay."

The monster gripped Abaven's face. "When I find whoever has it, they shall perish by my hand." Nurgal straightened and took a deep, steadying breath, as though the thought of destroying a rival soothed him. "Because if it is not in my hands, it is in the wrong ones."

I shuddered awake. Nurgal torturing Abaven. Had it been a dream? It didn't feel the same as the one I had about destroying the garden. That one had been a frightening possibility of an unavoidable future. My vision of Abaven in the cave had been tangible, as though I was right beside him. I wondered, if I could hear the thoughts of those who touched me when I was awake, could I stretch as far as the sky when I slept and see beyond Rós and Grania? Does the sky dream?

Lost in my thoughts, I almost didn't

notice that we had crested a wooded hill and were greeted by a vast, crystalline lake. From my perch on Rós's back, I watched her friend hesitate, seeing that even now she still fought every step of the journey. Yet here we were, surely at the end.

Grania stood there, beak agape, appearing overwhelmed by the vast size of the water and the mountainside soaring against it. The peaks cast their undisturbed reflection in the surface of the lake.

"We made it," Rós sighed. The white hen was silent. "Is everything alright, Grania?" Rós asked, perplexed at the inertia of her friend's colors.

"I did not think it would be so big."

"Why not?"

"Well, Wife always called the pigs' sty

a lake when it was muddy," Grania clucked.

Rós took in the majesty of the area. She loved how everything glowed. Every tree had its own unique color around it. The grass swayed in an oily way, blurred and green. The white caps on the mountains stood out against the stone gray, dotted by spring green trees. And the surface of the lake was as silver as the stars. "It's beautiful."

"How do we find the kelpie?" Grania asked after a moment.

An odd feeling settled over Rós, like pinfeathers growing in. Her mind clouded. "I suppose we let it find us."

Rós and Grania roamed the water's edge for days, both overcome with the same hazy sense of blitheness. Lost in a sublime trance, they eventually found themselves on the mountainside shore. It was unnaturally peaceful, eerily devoid of predators, yet teeming with other wildlife. Woodpeckers, abundant insects, and other peaceful creatures all roamed the area. The two hens wanted for nothing, and for a moment the memory of a farm life faded away.

"Remember the other place we used to live?" asked Grania one morning.

Rós slurped up a worm contentedly.

Grania stared across the lake where they had first arrived. "Do you think we should go back to it?"

"Why would we ever go back?" Rós clucked and dashed after a dragonfly.

Grania sighed. "Something about eggs."

"I laid three this morning. You can have them."

The morning light struck the eggs in such a way that they appeared golden. "Wait. What do I need eggs for?" Grania asked.

The red hen snapped at the air, trying to catch the dragonfly. "Clucks if I know.

We're wild chickens." The dragonfly zigzagged and landed on the water, sending out a ripple across the lake. Rós plunged her beak in after it. She soon forgot her pursuit and began drinking the water. Never had anything tasted so good. Cool, clear, crisp. Like fresh, melted snow.

The ripple reached the center of the lake and reverberated back in a curious manner. Rós's eyes fixed on a crest splitting the water, racing toward her.

"Rós, watch out!" Grania screeched.

Before the red hen could react, something bumped into her beak. She gulped, wide-eyed. Slowly a green horse head rose, muzzle pressed to Rós's beak. It blinked with sea-blue eyes beneath a tangle of bulrush mane and forelock, glowing with a bipolar layer of crimson and mantis green. It was in a constant shift between the two.

The red hen's heart hammered as she

snapped free from the magic of the lake. She could scarcely draw breath. *What do I say?*

I heard the creature's thoughts, for as much as I touched Rós, she touched the kelpie. It was a continual line.

The kelpie snorted. *I am drawn to that which does not belong to you.*

I wished to reach out and respond, but believed deeply that this was something Rós needed to face on her own. Her little mind raced. I silently willed her to say something.

"Hello," she said.

The kelpie squealed and rounded, crashing through the water. It bumped its head against the hen, nudging her playfully. I cannot fully express the relief that I felt beneath Rós's feathers. Where her vanes had been stiff before, tremulous even, they now softened and relaxed. I sensed an energy, a shift in her, that gave away how glad she was to have broken the ice.

"Are you the kelpie of Lake Lomond? Do you speak as I do?" she asked.

No, but I hear you. Do you hear me? the kelpie nickered.

Rós gasped. Her beak opened, tongue undulating as she received the kelpie's thoughts.

Oh, you do. You really do!

"How are you doing that?"

All base creatures share a singular language known as Root Tongue.

"Is that how I hear you?"

Yes, and I think the seed hears you, too.

Rós peered over her shoulder to me. "It's a piece of sky."

The kelpie pulled itself further on to shore to get a better view. *Is it now?*

"It fell like a star and struck me in the head." The hen looked to the creature.

"Now I see colors around all living things. I do not understand what the colors are."

That is interesting. What do you know about that piece of sky?

"Well…" Rós glanced at Grania who trotted to her side. "We were hoping you could tell us about it."

Picking up on her cue, Grania chimed in. "You see, we've asked others…. I think." She tilted her head to her friend, speaking in a hush. "Did we ask others?"

"Yes, I believe so. It's coming back to me now."

Grania stared across the vast lake in a stupor, then shook her head as if to free herself.

Rós plucked me from her back and presented me to the kelpie. "Do you know anything about it?"

The kelpie pressed its muzzle to my shell, its nostrils expanding and contracting. The heat of its breath fogged over me. Then things got fuzzy and dark with a dash of saliva. I tumbled back and forth. From behind a set of teeth, I caught glimpses of the chickens frantically running in circles.

"Do... not... eat... it!" Rós cried intermittently.

The kelpie was of no danger to me, for it rolled me on to the damp grass after inspection. Sunlight dried me quickly. I felt a little violated. What was with all these creatures trying to consume me?

I wasn't eating it, said the kelpie. It nudged me back to Rós who picked me up quickly, but with tremendous care. The kelpie continued as the hen placed me in the special spot on her back. *I have seen much within your sky. There is a dark force at work. The world is about to change, and you, little red hen, are at the center of it.*

"I?" Rós bawked. "But why me? I am just one chicken."

The seed, your piece of sky, has chosen you. What you have is precious and must not fall into the wrong hands. You must seek out the Great Hawk at the top of the mountain. The kelpie's gaze soared toward the peaks. The hens' followed. *The Great Hawk will be able to help you get the sky to safety.*

The kelpie slid back on the bank.

"Wait!" Rós squawked. "What happens if it falls into the wrong hands? What will it do?"

The kelpie wordlessly sank below the water, disappearing with no more than a blink.

Rós stared at Grania. "What do we do?"

"I think we should go home."

"Grania, this is something really big. What if we're the only ones who can stop it?"

"I want to go home. Why do you need to pursue this any further? The kelpie told us nothing. It did not even speak."

"It spoke to me!" Rós huffed, her frustration palpable. "The kelpie said the piece of sky needs to be taken to safety. I have to continue on."

"You don't have to be a hero, Rós. Come home with me."

"Grania, I don't want to be a hero. I just need to know our world is going to be alright."

The white hen shivered. "What if that acorn is what you say? What if it's something more than you can handle? What if," she bawked, "what if you…"

"What if I never come home?"

Grania bobbed her head, her expression pained.

"It's a real possibility." Rós blinked. "But what if it's worth it?"

"I'm afraid."

Rós shook out her feathers. "I know. To be honest, so am I."

Grania's whole body was etched with the strain of the journey. "I can't take another step. I'm going home."

"But I can't do this without you."

"I'm not cut out for this, Rós. You wanted to go on this journey. So go."

"Fine. Go home." Rós's heart sank. "It's not safe for hens like you anyway." She adjusted me on her back and squared her wings. "Be a chicken, you big sheep." She scanned the peaks behind them, refusing to look at the white hen. "Mind the kelpie, and those foxes… and that clucking log. I'll be keeping those eggs, too."

Grania stiffened as the words pelted her. She inhaled shakily and turned, hanging her head as she trudged away.

I didn't need to see Rós's eyes to sense the pain in her. Sometimes we say things out of hurt, or fear, or anger. Things we don't mean. When she turned away from Grania, she never looked back.

We found a path leading up the mountain and picked our way over it. The lake grew smaller behind us while a storm brewed far away and closed in. There was little shelter to be had, and we were hit hard by snow. I wished I could have warmed her somehow. Wished I was strong enough to brave growing again, so that I could tangle her within my vines and protect her like a shell, but I was still so small.

We froze to one another when Rós collapsed half-way up the mountain. The last thing I remember is a colossal shadow overtaking us.

VALLEYS BELOW

I dreamt of Abaven.

He was still in the cave, caged like an animal in a black iron cell. Welts of purple, yellow, and blue darkened his swollen eye, ribs, and shoulder. He trembled when he moved. Torchlight writhed on the cave walls. My vision wasn't hazy like before. It was clear, as though I was only a few feet away from him. I sensed a strong connection. He stared between the bars right through me. A thin line of dried blood split his lip. Where was Nurgal?

Abaven reached into the corner behind him and pulled out a bone, no bigger than Rós's leg, that jutted sharply at one end. He knelt behind the lock and angled his arm beneath it, shoving the broken end of the bone into the keyhole. He pressed his shoulder against the bars, trying to get better leverage, and carefully twisted and jimmied the bone. Beads of sweat formed at his temples. I noticed his clothes were ragged and filthy. He grunted with frustration. At last the lock clicked and the door swung open.

Abaven fell forward. He lay on the ground, not quite defeated, but not entirely triumphant. He lifted his face, and I watched his eyes scan the cave. Then, suddenly, I saw through them. They fixed on a sword hilt mounted on the wall. Inching forward arm over arm, we pulled toward it, hissing with discomfort. It took a great deal of effort to reach the wall where the sword rested. We managed to pull ourself up, legs spanning apart like roots of a tree. Our hand reached for the hilt. No sooner had we gripped it than a blaze of fire licked the blade.

We stared at the light, resolute.

I awoke to stillness.

The howling blizzard wind had ceased. I wasn't frozen anymore either.

It slowly sank in that I was not resting on Rós's back. Instead, something rough and bumpy wrapped around my shell. I sensed a broad claw, but it was not Nurgal's. No, this was a different beast entirely. Where was Rós?

I reached out to her. I had to know she was still there.

Rós, I said.

No answer.

If you are there, wake up.

Silence.

Rós, can you hear me?

And then, unexpectedly, a singular sweet thought reached back to me. *Are you my conscience?*

I'd recognize her voice anywhere. *No. I'm a piece of sky. What's a conscience?*

Who told you you were a piece of sky?

You did. You called me Little Sky, I said.

Little Sky? Wait. I sensed her confusion. *You can talk?*

I can talk!

Why have you not spoken before?

You hurled me at Grania.

Just the once, Rós replied.

You let dog lick me.

He was trying to help.

Horse snot. I sulked.

If it's any consolation, I was exceptionally concerned when the kelpie had you in its mouth.

That reminds me. You wanted to eat me.

Rós went quiet. *Only the one time. I would never eat you, Little Sky.*

Not even a bite?

Not one bite.

A third voice interjected. *I, also, shall not eat either of you.*

The darkness broke around me, and I stared up into the face of a massive white bird, ten times the size of the little red hen. I shrank in my shell, until I saw Rós who stared up in wonder at the creature. Their eyes met.

"Are you my mother?" Rós asked softly.

The creature blinked, easing its clutch around the chicken who got up and began inspecting him. I rested soundly in the other claw. We lay by a snow drift at the mountain's peak, but we were so high that clouds blocked the view of the valley.

"No," it said in a deep, bemused baritone. The beast rose slowly and I watched Rós get another look.

She trotted around, gaping. Grand wings rested over fur the color of the snow around us, touched at the tips with black like mountain stone. Rós's perplexed expression told me she was having trouble piecing this together. "You are one very large dog."

"I am last of my kind."

"Paws and haunches like dog, big like The Mare, but the rest like myself." Rós cocked her head. "You are a very strange looking dog. But I like the colors swirling around you. You almost blend into the sky with that shade of blue."

"I am a gryphon," the beast chortled. "I am he they call the Great Hawk. My name is Shiver, and I am the last of my kind. I found you freezing on the mountainside."

Rós glanced to me and crossed to the place I rested. "This is a piece of the sky, and the kelpie of the lake below said that you would know how to get it to safety."

I'm dangerous, I bleated.

Shiver's green eyes bored into my core. *Only in the wrong hands.* He gazed at

A PIECE OF SKY

Rós. "Do you believe this piece of sky is dangerous?"

She blinked at me, and if I could hold my breath, I swear I would have.

"I think it is the most beautiful thing I've ever seen." She looked up at the gryphon. "And if it is dangerous, I do not fear it." Rós nudged me in his claw.

Shiver snapped his talon shut around me. "Good."

The hen squabbled in surprise.

"You are going to need courage for what is about to come."

Shiver screamed against the ever-clear mountain air. We lurched to the muffled beating of wings.

Have you ever had such an unnerving sense of fear that all you could do was screech with laughter?

As the gryphon relaxed his grip upon

me, holding me only tight enough to prevent me from falling, I saw Rós in his other claw. She had an expression of sheer exhilaration. The air rippled over her feathers, and she stretched out her neck, working her wings free.

Shiver readjusted his hold on her to keep her safe, but gave her the rein she desired. She spread her wings. Her thoughts were so joyful, so full of laughter, they boomed within me. *I'm flying!*

Not okay, NOT OKAY! I screamed inside. I wished Shiver would hold me tighter. My place was on the ground, not up here above Lake Lomond. I noticed the way it split and forked through the forest around it, shining like silver veins in a flesh of evergreen. The trees flung themselves half way up the gray mountains in a scattered kind of desperation. Early morning sunlight dashed against us from the horizon, while streaks of pink and orange warmed the hillside.

A sense of beauty forced its way into me. Is this what the sky felt like? Did it marvel to view the whole world this way? To reach beyond with hopeful endlessness. That moment of fear that can only be stifled by laughter made me wish that I could laugh with Rós, for I thought one bubbled up in me. I stole a little bravery, and quelled the fear within.

"This is every chicken's dream," Rós cackled over the roar of air. She closed her eyes. I thought I glimpsed a smile, if chickens could smile. She opened her beak, tongue undulating, as though to taste the sweet air around us.

Where are you taking us? I asked.

To an old friend, Shiver responded. *It would take months for your friend to walk, and time is not something we have. Is it, Little Sky?*

I pulled back the tendrils within me

that begged to get out. While I could not deny the beauty I felt, I was also having a harder time resisting the urge to grow. In one day, I could destroy the world.

What is the matter? Shiver asked. *I thought you were a piece of sky. Why do you fear being near it?*

I felt blank. I was a piece of sky, and I was afraid of heights. No words came to me.

I do not think you are afraid of the height. I think you are afraid of soaring. He let out a call and banked left. *My friend will know your true desire, as I sense it now.*

Rós squirmed excitedly at the sudden shift in altitude. Shiver cried in return and rolled in a tight spiral, his talons scraping the sky. He tossed Rós, allowing her to glide through the air like her flight-borne cousins, then caught her again. I hoped he never did that to me. It made me sick to watch. Now more than ever, I wanted to be on the ground.

I wanted to be rooted.

We landed in a heavily-wooded grove far from the mountains. Rós took me up at once and strode next to Shiver. The gryphon kept his eyes fixed ahead. On what, I wasn't sure yet.

The grove teemed with wildlife. Deer and rabbits who had been grazing burst into motion, bounding by. Squirrels zipped up tree trunks. A woodpecker throttled a tree. Water babbled nearby in song. A deep sense of life drenched the air, seeping into my shell. Filling me with joy.

At the center of the grove was an ancient tree as big as the god oak. I sensed Rós's heart quickening. A single thought rippled through her as she stared.

GINORMOUS!

Excitement filled me as we approached. It was a sensation as though I was about to be reunited with an old friend. But how could that be when I knew no other tree than the god oak?

Shiver bowed before the tree. "Cerennunos, awaken."

What did he just say? Rós asked me privately.

Cerennunos, awaken.

What's a serren you knows?

The tree groaned deeply. Large lips and eyes pressed through the bark. A nose like Abaven's appeared. The tree smacked its mouth, as though sleep had left a dry taste. It squinted at the gryphon. "Shiver?"

"Hello, old friend."

Cerennunos smiled. "What brings you to my part of the woods?"

Shiver nodded to the hen beside him. "I brought friends."

I swung from Rós's beak, just as awed as she was. Her breath caught. *Clucks alive! I've never seen a talking tree. Wait. I thought you said he had a cere on his nose?*

I said Cerennunos, I murmured.
Did you just sneeze?

Cerennunos squinted. "What is it you have there?"

Rós laid me on the forest floor. Had I not been so taken with Cerennunos, I would have burrowed into the ground at once and never let go. I wanted to live in this place. It was perfect. "Hello… sir, is it?" Rós clucked. "This is a piece of the sky. It hit me in the head, and now I see colors. I came an awfully long way to show it to you."

Cerennunos's lips pursed. "Bring it closer."

Rós plucked me from the ground and trotted up to the tree. I trembled to be this close to such a force of nature.

"Shiver." The tree turned his eyes to the gryphon after examining me for a long while. "Do you realize what this is?"

"Yes, my lord."

"You were right in bringing it here."

Shiver bowed his head.

The tree looked again to Rós and I. "What I am about to tell you, no man can know."

Rós inhaled sharply. I would have too.

"Shiver introduced me as Cerennunos."

"Umm," said the hen, "I thought I heard one of you say there's a cere on your wren's nose. I don't see any wrens, aaaaaand…." Her head cocked. "You're a tree. Trees don't have ceres. *Birds* have ceres. I don't see one on you. Is there a wren you know?"

The tree chuckled. "My *name* is Cerennunos. I am the Father of the Forest. What you have there is the most powerful force in all of creation. There is a creature out there far worse than any have dreamed before whose sole desire is to overthrow the earth and rule in an everlasting world of green. All living things, save for the creature and the world he creates, would be choked from existence. My children, Tree Folk of the Summer Isle, live in fear of the one who calls himself Nurgal. So deep is their fear that they wish to overthrow me, so that they may obey the Lord of Decay and have peace once again. But the peace they seek is an eternal one from which they would never recover. The kind man experiences when he is no longer a part of our world."

That was an awful lot to take in.

"Nurgal is coming." The tree continued, "In his hands, the seed you hold could kill us all."

I was afraid he would say that.

"But it's not in Nurgal's hands, is it? No. It's in yours, little one. And even though you are only one soul, you hold the power to change the world. You can stop Nurgal. You can change our fates. For as much destruction your piece of sky can cause, it can also bring life. It's happened before, you know. The battle for the seed is in constant motion. Long ago, such a seed was won by the Creator. The world flourished. And is it not beautiful?"

Shiver carefully took me from Rós's beak and nestled me in my favorite place on her back. "The world is a glorious place," he said softly. "I wouldn't want anything to change it."

Cerennunos sighed. "We have a shared responsibility with man. They the keepers of the earth, and I the Father of the Forest. I fear they have lost sight of this great responsibility. Balance has been disrupted. Nurgal marches against them."

"Is there hope? Can balance be restored?" Shiver asked.

Cerennunos regarded him, then us. "I believe mankind can right itself with guidance. It is never too late to do the right thing."

"What must we do?" Rós asked.

Cerennunos's eyes narrowed. "You must go to the land of the Fae. You must call them to our aid."

"How do we get there?"

"Find the veil."

A FAULT IN THE STARS

8

We stayed with Cerennunos that night. He made us feel safe, although we now knew that Nurgal could arrive at any time. Isn't it funny how someone can make you feel safe, even when disaster is moments away?

Many questions spilled from the little red hen with the setting of the sun. I can't remember them all, but Cerennunos found her candor amusing.

"Say it one more time," she pleaded.

"Cerennunos," said the tree.

Rós cackled as though it was the funniest thing she had ever heard.

"Why is it funny?"

"Because there's no cere on your nose."

"I haven't seen wrens in a while either."

Rós sobered. "Do you think Nurgal has anything to do with that? Could he scare them away?"

"Nurgal has caused much fear. Even my Tree children are beginning to bow. It's a powerful thing, you know. Fear can do so much more harm to one person than any other state of being."

"It's true," Shiver said. "I can't tell you how many times I froze on my mountain while learning to fly. I wasn't always brave."

Rós glanced his way. "What changed?"

"I figured out that bravery is not the absence of fear. It is courage in the face of it."

"Which is why I wish my children would show some bark," Cerennunos sighed. "They bend to wickedness."

"Speaking of bark." Rós said, "Dog says

E.N.T. stands for evil neurotic trees."

"He must have misunderstood. As you can see I am not evil or neurotic, and I am father to them all. Naturally, we are a peaceful race. I think it is the evil in the world that has made them neurotic. I believe Nurgal's touch makes them…. What is the word I seek?" Cerennunos's eyes turned upward. He smacked his mouth as though the word were on the tip of his tongue. "Necrotic. His sickness kills."

"Why are they working for Nurgal?" Shiver asked. "What can he offer them that they don't already have?"

Cerennunos sighed. "I fear when he touches them, it destroys the good inside. As though they have given up their agency. It breaks my heart to see them like this."

Rós turned her head. "You have a heart?"

"You sound surprised."

"Well, I see your colors. That is a nice wildflower purple on you, by the way. It really compliments the gold surrounding it. But your heart…?"

All Father Trees have hearts, I offered. *Some manifest it differently than others.*

"I feel as though mine beats deepest of all," said Cerennunos. "I try to warn them that Nurgal will never show mercy. When he gets what he wants, it will be the end of us. They believe the only way to win back their peace is to do his bidding and silence me."

Rós turned to gaze at me. *We must be sure that never happens.*

Shiver kept Rós and me warm in the darkness. The little red hen nestled close to the beast. I sensed a hurting in her heart softened by his closeness. Grania had left her a bit sore. I learned that when you lose someone special to you, you don't only hurt inside, but outside too. Your whole body changes, like a piece of you has gone missing. I sometimes felt that way about Abaven.

As Rós slept, I worried about what Cerennunos had said. That I was powerful, and in the wrong hands—dangerous. But I wasn't in the wrong hands. I was with Rós. She seemed so fearless to me, so completely unafraid to be herself. She knew who and what she was, and didn't expect anything more. She lived an unapologetic existence.

Have you ever had the feeling you were being watched? I would describe the sensation as prickly, the way a ragged leaf feels when brushed over one's shell. That sensation crawled over me. When I looked in the direction of the feeling, I found Shiver gazing at me. He spoke to me through thought so as not to wake the little red hen.

You seem bothered.
I am, I confessed.
What has you perplexed?

I wished I could sigh. Sighing would have made me feel so much better. *I want to grow, but I am afraid of what will happen to the earth if I do. Is this what it feels like to be torn?*

Shiver turned his eyes to the sky. I guess he didn't want to talk after all.

Sorry, I mumbled.

Do not apologize for who you are. He looked at me briefly, then back towards the sky. *Look at the stars. They don't apologize for being what they are.*

Enormous balls of burning gas?

He chortled quietly. *You're funny. I like you.*

Gee, thanks, I said back with more sarcasm than I meant.

He preened his feathers for a moment, then turned his eyes back toward the night. *For centuries, man has gazed at a heaven overflowing with stars, and wondered why those skyward jewels move our souls, why they fill us with wonder and hope.*

Definitely not gas, I mumbled.

Shiver returned his gaze to me, studying me for an uncomfortable amount of time. I wanted to burrow beneath Rós's feathers and hide. His voice was gentle, but firm, like the final falling of leaves that heralds the winter. *War is coming. And it isn't about good or evil, or whether the world will end or not…*

It's about **YOU**.

Should Nurgal gain control of you, you will have to decide who you are. Are you a piece of the sky, surrounded by the divine light that makes man yearn for eternity— or an acorn?

Rós thinks I'm a piece of sky.

The opinions of others matter not, Shiver stated.

It matters who you believe you are.

How will I know who I truly am? I asked.

Each of his words fell quietly with growing strength.

Your potential is infinite, and when you realize that, you'll have your answer. You have a purpose in this world that will define you.

I stared at the stars. Like them, I was limitless.

Shiver curled his claws beneath his proud, downy breast, and tucked his head beneath his wing. *Think on that*, he admonished. *I can offer you no better armor or weapon than that knowledge, for I will be gone come morning.*

As he settled into a deep slumber, I wondered what Abaven would do.

I saw through his eyes that night.

Flaming sword in hand, we strode from the cave, bracing against the mouth of it. The sun was beginning to peek over the horizon, and I felt as though our stare fixed on the grove. His heart pounded, thoughts clear. Somewhere out there was the most powerful force on earth, and he was going to find it. I swelled within at the thought of being reunited with him.

But then our eyes cast downward, skimming across the valley, and took in the carnage Nurgal had left behind. Scorched earth, decaying trees, a poisoned Lake Lomond in the distance.

The path of destruction swept in the direction of the grove. A clearly visible army of corrupted Tree Folk grew larger mile by mile as they fell in behind Nurgal, marching onward with no reprieve. The grief we felt was unequivocal.

Abaven stole a little courage and began down the mountain.

He was coming.

And so was Nurgal.

Little Sky...

Her voice drifted through my nightmare, showing me the way out. Like a light in the dark, she grounded me back in reality.

"Little Sky, it's me, Rós."

Hello, I said.

"Good morning."

The grove we had bedded down in for the night rematerialized. Cerennunos must have been sleeping, for the great tree was faceless like any other. Shiver was nowhere in sight. We were alone. The last time we were on our own, we nearly died. I shuddered.

"Are you alright?" She pressed her beak to me until I calmed. "Sometimes at night, I feel you tremble. The way you did just now."

You heard them say what I am. How can I not cower when they all tell me I'm dangerous?

The little red hen tucked her beak

under her wing, and me snug beneath it. She spoke softly. "They said you are powerful. Nurgal is dangerous." She hugged me closer. "There's a difference."

I have dreamed what I am capable of, and it frightens me.

She clucked softly, sounding amused.

Why are you laughing?

"It's funny that I dream of the sky, and the sky dreams of the earth."

Silence stuck in me.

"You are such a little thing, and yet capable of so much," she said. "Do not fear the power in you, for I think it is a beautiful thing. I won't let Nurgal get you. We won't let the earth overgrow."

I thought of my first dream. Twisting around the god oak, choking it. Separating from it to crush Abaven, only to escape from the garden and poison the earth, annihilating everything in my path. I remembered how I had not been able to quell that urge to grow once planted. *What if I can't stop?*

It was hard for me to allow what I had dreamed to touch her mind. I feared she would abandon me for it. But Rós was no ordinary hen. She tensed at first, but then fought back the dream, and I was filled with a vision of how she saw the world. The glorious sunrise we had shared with Shiver while airborne, the veins of silver water pulsing through the evergreens, and everything haloed by the glow of life I had caused her to see when I crashed into her on that fated stormy night. All of the world, flourishing before us, alive and green. Her voice filled me.

I hope you never stop.

"Excuse me?" Rós asked Cerennunos whose trunk showed no signs of ever having had a face. "Sir?" She walked around him, pecking his trunk gently.

"Hello?" Her feathers ruffled. "Sir Wren You Knows?"

No response.

"Hey!" She pecked harder. "You with the funny name."

I think he's gone back to sleep, Little Sky mumbled. *And I don't think he appreciates you poking his Oon-nod.*

"His... what?"

Nevermind.

"You're making that up."

Am not.

"What's an Oon-nod anyway? Do I have one?"

It's... erm... a tree thing.

"Sky." Rós shook her head. "I bet there's no such thing as an Oon-nod." She turned her attention back to Cerennunos. "I was hoping to ask him for directions to the veil." She raised her foot and scratched the bark on the trunk in a final effort. When nothing happened, she sighed. "I guess we're on our own."

Why didn't she think to ask how to find the veil he spoke of before they had bedded down last night? Was it like the cloth Farmer's wife dotted against her face in the summer heat? Or was it a vale like the valley that cradled the farm?

While she wasn't sure she could find something that she didn't know looked like, she remained confident she would find it. She had to. She'd made a promise to the piece of sky. It needed to believe it could change the world in a magnificent way, because Rós wanted to believe such a thing was possible with doom lurking.

She regretted not asking the tree what to look for. A clue, anything. She began thinking of what she knew about finding things.

Well, sometimes she found bugs hiding under ground. Perhaps the veil would hide down there too.

So she began scratching. Which turned into digging. And eating. Bugs were delicious, and blast if she wasn't hungry. She began to sing as she dug herself into a hole as deep as Dog was long and tall.

> Here comes the chicken to save the day!
> I'll find it somehow.
> We'll be okay.
> Cuz out there somewhere
> Is the Fae,
> But I don't have all egging day.
> Can anyone tell me
> What's a Fae?
> Clucks if I know.
> Who's to say?
> Forces of evil... kept at bay.
> Today's a super duper chicken finding veils sort of day!

Rós surveyed the hole around her. Her eyes barely peered over the edge. She peeked over her shoulder to check on the piece of sky, and ground her beak in thought. *Hmmm…*

A PIECE OF SKY

"I may have gone a bit overboard on this hole." The trees swayed gently in a breeze, causing the dappled light on the forest floor to dance. Her eyes darted back and forth. "Little Sky, do you see a way out?"

Don't ask me. I don't have eyes.

"Neither does the sky, but it sees the entire world."

Why would I see a way out of a hole you dug?

"Oh, I don't know," Rós clucked. "Because you're a piece of sky."

I don't think the veil is down here.

"Are you alright? You sound a little grumpy."

Being beneath the soil like this makes me nervous. Can you dig a little around the edges and form a slope?

Rós was game to try. She started at one end of the hole, and pulled dirt toward her, but the hole just got longer. She huffed and ran to a side, trying again. The hole got wider. "I don't think it's working."

Could you take the dirt you have and pile it up?

Oh! Rós clucked. She ran to one of the sides she hadn't pulled dirt from and sized it up, then ran to the piles of dirt and began pushing them. She gathered enough to make a soft pile.

Though she sank with each step, leaving criss-crossed hatch-marky footprints in the mounds, she managed to get close enough to the top of the hole, nail her beak into the forest floor, and pull herself up with a squabble and a flap of the wings. She lay on her side panting, with the piece of sky tucked near her shoulder.

"We did it." Rós gathered her breath and found her feet. She wondered what else she could try. What else did she know about finding things? She sauntered over to a tree and pecked it.

A PIECE OF SKY

Ow! said the piece of sky.

Rós jumped and ran in a small circle. "I'm so sorry. Did that hurt you? I didn't mean to hurt you. Wait." She paused. "How did that hurt *you?* I didn't peck you."

The tree said 'Ow.' It would appreciate if you didn't do that again.

Rós circled the offended tree and gazed into its high branches. "Sorry about that."

The tree creaked softly, rattling its leaves. The little red hen awed at how the colors around it changed before her from an offended, mistrusting dragonfly green to lightning blue.

He says 'You're forgiven.'

"I never want to hurt anyone." She backed away and tried pecking a rock. Maybe the veil was in the rock.

The rock would also appreciate it if you did not attack it.

Rós zipped about in a fretted circle of

frustration.

I think we need to think bigger than scratching holes and pecking things, said the little sky.

Rós sighed. "I think you're right." She looked around. "Think bigger." Her eyes wandered up and down trees, between them, over moss-covered boulders, over bushes.

Bigger, whispered the piece of sky.

Rós's eyes trailed to the sky. The cogs in her head cranked hard. The sky. The. Sky. She thought of the piece of sky on her back. "Golden eggs, THE SKY!"

Bingo.

"But how do we get up there?"

Clucks if I know, the little sky pipped.

Rós glanced over her shoulder in wonder.

It spoke innocently. *What?*

She ground her beak and half-closed her eyes in amusement. "You're a funny looking chicken, Little Sky."

A PIECE OF SKY

You see colors around everything, of course I look funny to you.

She shrugged her wings, repositioning the piece of sky. The roar of water in the near distance trundled over the air.

"Do you hear that?" Rós strode forward, following the sound, taking in the colors around her. The trees seemed to have their own personality, glowing with blue, lavender, or silver around their trunks and limbs. Some animals passing by exuded yellow or pink.

Rós broke from the line of trees, stepping onto large, white and silver rocks. A clear stream of water wove between them. To her right, water cascaded over a high, mossy ledge, crowned by a misty rainbow. She thought she saw a cave behind it.

"Do you think it's an entrance? It's big, like the sky. The water sort of looks like a veil."

Let's find out.

She picked her way over to the rock shelf that jutted from the cliff. It went behind the waterfall. She peeked in, but it didn't appear to be anything special.

"Do you think we need to go through the water? There's a rainbow over it, maybe the water is magic."

Rós backed away from the mouth of the cave. A few rocks trailed beneath the bottom of the falls and inside the cavern. She hopped from one to the other. They were slippery and made it difficult to keep one's balance. She flapped a little so she didn't fall down.

Gazing at the water falling in a curtain, she dashed through with a deep breath. The water pounded her, and she came out drenched on the other side.

Have you ever seen a wet chicken? It's not pretty. Mainly because feathers make up more of the chicken than the chicken itself.

The water had not helped my problem. It had agitated it, and that feeling I dreaded, that feeling from my dream of not being able to stop myself from progressing, was imminent and immense.

When the water pelted me, I instantly reached out to hang on to my brave hen. I don't think either of us realized what I had done until she turned around to face the back of the falls.

The outline of a man stood on the other side. Rós caught glimpses of him and froze. At first she thought the water was distorting the colors around him, for she had only seen split colors on the kelpie. But when he passed beneath the water, it became clear.

A strong halo of white, like an

impenetrable wall, supported dual colors of purple on one side, and clay brown on the other. They clashed together like two spirits fighting for ownership over a man with silver hair, dark eyes, and pointed ears.

He was bruised and broken, dirty and tattered. He crouched, flaming sword sheathed in a makeshift scabbard of rawhide and gazed back. Rós didn't know whether to hide, or run up to the person. His colors were misleading.

He spoke aloud in the Root Tongue. "I am Abaven."

Hello, Rós said.

His eyes narrowed with scrutiny.

The little red hen's thoughts reached back to the piece of sky. *What do I do? I don't know whether to go forward or back.*

"I won't hurt you," Abaven said evenly. "I'm here to help. You and I both want the same thing." His eyes remained fixed on the damp breast of the hen. "Although, I think we may have a problem."

Rós followed his gaze and finally noticed the green tendrils wrapped around her neck.

"I think if it's growing, we're running out of time."

Rós, said the little sky, *he's right. I feel it in me. I don't know how much longer I can last. Either way, I have to grow.*

I don't know if I can trust him, Little Sky. His colors…. When I look at the purple, I feel his honor. But then there's the brown. She paused a moment, considering. *It's like there's something inside him that disagrees with itself. I don't know which way to lean.*

Rós took a deep breath and hesitantly stepped forward. *My name is Rós. We are trying to reach the Fae. Can you help us find the veil?*

Abaven nodded. "Tonight the stars align, and the veil will be its thinnest. Our worlds will join. Why do you need to cross it?"

The Father of the Forest has told us we must ask for the Fae's help. Life as we know it is at risk. Nurgal is coming.

Abaven's eyes fixed on the golden seed on Rós's back. His eyes shifted to hers quickly as if staring too long would raise suspicion. "I can take you to the queen."

He swallowed, fingers twitching as they rested on his knees. "You've done a wonderful job protecting the seed. I am sure she would want to meet you."

Rós watched the brown above him push back against the purple, taking a majority power. She stepped back.

The Fae guard straightened. "We need to move quickly. Come with me."

He left the cave and stood on the rocks outside.

Rós stalled.

We need to go, the piece of sky urged.

I know, but there's something about him. Are you sure he is trustworthy?

Do you have a choice?

A Piece of Sky

There is always a choice.

She finally crept around the falls and observed the Fae guard. He turned his face to a sky dotted with stars, then drew his sword and pointed it toward them. The blade jumped to life with fire. He slashed from one star to another. Rós's eyes widened as the constellations moved across the sky at his command. When the sky went indigo with night, a silver line streaked down the center, like a rift in the cosmos. It tore apart, opening on to a swirl of suns, worlds, and colors.

He looked at Rós and the piece of sky. "Time to go."

THE LAWS OF MAGIC
9

"Come forth, He who is named Abaven."

I'm not entirely sure how we got there. One moment we were in our world, rending the sky in two. The next, we stood in a dark, vast expanse, filled with rippling clouds of purple and teal. Stars of white, blue, and orange freckled the horizon. Thin pillars of soft gold rose through the clouds like the strings of a great harp. They vibrated when the voice spoke.

We followed Abaven forward. I found myself recoiling in my spot on Rós's back as her eyes filled with the universe around us.

The Fae guard took a knee before the pillars and bowed his head. "I am Abaven, first born of Araren, sent to guard the Father Tree, the tree of life."

The strings of gold vibrated again. "You failed at your assigned task. Nurgal captured the seed."

"I am sorry I have failed you in that respect, Queen Uonaidh, but the seed has been recovered." He motioned to the hen.

So that's an Oon-nod. Rós blinked blankly at the strings of light. *Sky, I take back what I said about you making that up. Your Oon-nod is very pretty.*

And all this time I thought I had one…

"What is this you bring me?" asked Uonaidh.

Though the voice addressed Abaven, I was keenly aware her focus was on me. I felt as though a part of her wrapped around me in deep examination. Her presence was even more powerful than

Abaven's. She possessed an inner light so strong, I felt unworthy to be within it. I shuddered, and tried to hide in the deepest corner of myself. *I'm dangerous. Flawed. I don't deserve to be here. I cannot share your light.*

I jolted into reverie. In this dark corner of myself was Nurgal. His imprint. Left behind from the one time he had possessed me. My vision was clear in the center, petering out at the edges. I was in the grove with Cerennunos. The great tree's eyes were wide with terror. But I didn't see it as though I were sitting beside him.

No.

I was Nurgal.

We stood before Cerennunos with squared shoulders, breathing deeply, evenly. As though what was about to happen would send waves of tremendous pleasure through the Lord of Decay.

I became aware of the sound of slow,

steady stomping gathering around us. From the edges of my sight, I saw an army of Evil Necrotic Trees amassing. Their branches and tree tops rustled with the breeze.

"Join us," Nurgal rumbled. "Together we can eradicate man. Wipe the earth clean. Renew again."

Cerennunos shook. "I am the Father of the Forest. I will not submit."

A sneer twisted Nurgal's face. He raised a hand and snapped his fingers. The Evil Necrotic Trees descended upon Cerennunos at once in a massive onslaught. They rocked him back and forth until his roots pulled from the earth.

And Nurgal laughed.

But then he became aware of the intruder inside. Me. And if I did not fear him before, I did now, for I heard his single thought clearly. *I see you.*

I jerked away from the shadows I hid in, bringing me back to the Fae world and the court of Queen Uonaidh.

Uonaidh's presence remained around me, her words meant only for me. *Who are you?*

I knotted up inside. *I am the reason the world will end.*

Rós's thoughts pushed past us. *Are you alright, Little Sky?*

I was relieved to hear her. She always seemed to save me at the right moment. *Yes,* I answered. *But not really.*

You will be okay. We are here together, remember? Abaven will help us.

"This low creature has protected the seed in my absence," said Abaven. "I wish you to recognize her as a guardian of our world. She has earned it."

"We shall see about that. Tell me, creature, what is it that you call yourself?"

The little red hen's heart pounded. She bawked her name. *Rós.*

"Tell me Rós, do you know the laws of magic?"

Rós blinked. *Laws?*

"The laws of magic are basic rules all living kind must obey. There are seven in total. You need know only three— the Law of Knowledge: One who understands power, controls power. the Law of Names: One who knows a true name controls it. Base creatures, such as yourself, understand Root Tongue. It is how you can hear me now. To know a true name is to control it, no matter the element."

Rós tensed. *Do you know what is happening to my world?*

"Nurgal wishes to destroy it. We know man is worth saving. We need man as much as man needs us, even if they do not realize it."

And these laws you speak of, why do I need to know them?

"We wish you to know these laws in order to arm you against Nurgal. To have knowledge is to have power. The third law you must understand pertains to the seed you carry. It is the Law of Balance: One must not gain or lose too much power at the peril of their lives. Should Nurgal gain the seed, balance will be broken."

You tell me these things, but why does it sound like you will not be helping?

At that moment, another personage similar to Abaven entered the space. The other Fae was dressed simply, as though he were a servant. He approached the pillars of light confidently and began speaking in a language that Rós and I did not understand. Abaven tensed beneath the paling of his face. His hands balled into fists.

The pillars were still as they listened to the messenger. He cast a look of disgust and wariness toward my Fae guardian. Abaven swallowed hard, face drawn, and glanced to Rós. "We should go," he whispered.

No. Rós pecked his hand. *Will you not*

help us? she demanded of Uonaidh.

No answer.

Please say something, the hen begged.

Abaven scooped her up, despite her squabbling and wiggles. She got a wing free and flapped hard, struggling against him. He smoothed a hand over her neck and back. I shivered as his hand passed over me. It was not the touch I had been expecting all of this time.

Abaven turned his back on Uonaidh and marched away. Rós squawked in distress. Her anger and fear radiated through her feathers. The Fae guardian swung his sword, opening a doorway to a darkened stone corridor, lined with braziers of fire. They cast his shadow five times his height, and darkened his already gaunt features. He set Rós down and crouched before us.

"Give me the acorn."

Rós gawked at him. *It's a piece of sky.*

"It would be safer here with us. If we have it, Nurgal does not. The damage he can do without it is minimal."

They call him Lord of Decay. I have a feeling the world would still be in a bad way with him skulking about.

Abaven took a slow breath, as if to steady his temper. "Give. Me. The. Acorn."

Rós watched the brown around him consume the purple. The white wall beneath the colors grew thicker. She took a step back. *No.*

The Fae guard rose, flaming sword at the ready. "We can do this the easy way, or the hard way, little hen. Give me the acorn, and you live. Take another step back, and your life is at peril."

She scratched the floor defiantly. *My life has been in peril from the moment the sky fell. I'm still here.* She rounded. *You strike no fear in me!* And dashed.

Abaven was after her at once.

Rós squabbled and squawked, leaving behind a trail of feathers. *Why do you want the sky so badly?*

She skittered around a corner so hard and fast, the piece of sky tumbled from her back… right into Abaven's hands.

BAD SEED

When Abaven swung his sword, the little red hen vanished. This was not the guardian I knew. There was a hardness around his heart, a pain he kept shielded. I felt it in the heaviness of his shoulders. He dropped his guard momentarily. I reached into his mind, hoping I would find madness. I could forgive madness.

I found a memory.

Two creatures of shadow dragged him from the iron cell he'd been kept in, and threw him before Nurgal. The Fae guard lay on the ground, heavily beaten. A broken man.

Nurgal paced. "I give you one last

chance. Retrieve what I desire."

"Why would I ever help you?" Abaven wheezed. "You'll kill me either way."

"You want to know what's in it for you? What the Lord of Decay might possibly offer someone with notions of honor and all that drivel. Well…." He took a seat upon a throne in a corner. "I'll allow you to live, for starters."

A thought went through Abaven's mind so quickly that I could not follow. A shift. His eyes flashed. "If I'm going to live in disgrace, I'm going to need more than that."

"A deputy in my ranks."

Abaven rose, legs quaking. "Who are you fooling, Nurgal? We both know no one is going to be around after you gain control."

Nurgal growled and leaned his chin upon his fist. "You would be the last remaining Fae, a king, elevated beyond all others."

"Kings die as well."

The sound of the sinewy vines flexing in Nurgal was emphasized by the intimacy of the cave. "You would be as Cerennunos, Father to All. The gate keeper. The Lord of all that Lasts. We could have a partnership, you and I. All I need is the seed."

Abaven smirked. "A god. Now we're talking."

I broke from Abaven's mind, horror stricken. It couldn't be true. Why would he commit such utter betrayal? I shrank within myself, determined more than ever before not to allow the world to be twisted beneath the will of these individuals.

As I tried to hide away from him in the deepest corner of my shell, I took on the Lord of Decay's sight with a fear I didn't know I had. I had gone to that place where his imprint was, where there was total darkness, and a sense of self-loathing. I hated this spiraling out of control, bouncing from one consciousness to the next, but I couldn't stop.

Nurgal was curled around Cerennunos, whom the Evil Necrotic Trees had partially uprooted, and melded to the trunk. Vines from his body wrapped around the few roots that remained, yanking them from the earth.

Cerennunos choked and gasped. Creatures fell dead around him. The soil turned black and spread before him like a plague. Spidery scarlet seams scrawled across the newly bare earth, pulsing with infection.

Nurgal's own roots raced along with the scourge, and I witnessed his solitary truth— his idea of a perfect world, where all died from his sickness. Creatures and men both turned to bone, then dust, nourishing the viny buds that were part of Nurgal.

And there he was at the center of it

all, having turned himself into his own version of a Father Tree, becoming one with Cerennunos into a single Tree of Death, and everything it came in contact with withered.

The world was green, yes, but there was no beauty to it. The world lay absolutely still. There was peace, but it was from silence so thick it was thunderous.

Nurgal's thoughts were clear. *Man is a plague, a blemish upon the earth. An infestation.*

The last I saw of his vision of the Tree of Death was a black acorn swinging from a limb.

I don't know what happened after that. I think I blacked out….

Yeah, I'm pretty sure I blacked out.

Where was Rós? Where had Abaven sent her? I felt as though I had been cut from her, like the time I fell from the god oak. Without Rós, I couldn't tell if I was a piece of sky or not. All I knew was that I was a seed, and a bad one at that. I couldn't even decide if I wanted to grow or not, not that I had a choice.

I tried to remember the world Rós wanted, the one where the sun rose in glory, the early spring air whistled by and kissed your face, and kelpies and gryphons played. The kind of world where chickens fly, and no one questions their motives about wanting to cross paths.

The time had come that Shiver spoke of, where I must decide if I am a piece of sky or a lowly seed. I wasn't afraid of what the world would become. I wasn't afraid of what Nurgal would do to me. For too long, I had been afraid of soaring. I feared my potential. No matter what the morning brought, I would fear it no longer.

Rós was right all along.

THE CHOSEN ONE
II

Rós opened her eyes in a half-lidded stupor. Her head pounded. She waited for her eyes to adjust, for all they saw were millions of blurred colors. She rose dizzily, but collapsed. *Where am I? What happened?*

She had an odd sense that this had all occurred before, as though in a dream. A sound scraped through her head, similar to when Farmer sharpened his axe. She gathered her feet beneath her again and staggered. When she was steady, she glanced over her shoulder. Something had changed. Something was missing.

Then she remembered.

Laws of magic.
      A flaming sword.
            The acorn.
    No… **The Sky.**

Her heart surged. Air stuck in her lungs. *Little Sky!*

Her body followed her head frantically like when Dog chases his tail. *It's lost.*

She took a deep breath to steady her panic. *Alright. Where am I, really?*

Recognition settled in. She had been here before on the night of the storm. This was the outskirts of the farm. She stood close to the hill where she had first seen the Tree Folk. Perhaps a better view from higher ground might help her find the piece of sky. Maybe it would call for her. She glanced up, half expecting it to sail toward her, because what she saw was much like the night they met.

A swirling mass of purple clouds lingered over whatever lay beyond that hill. Lightning flashed out of the black, void-like center. Rós scratched one foot, then the other, and shook out her feathers before taking that hill.

She careened up it in madness, free and with abandon. Her breath raced, heart pounding, when she crested the top. The vortex darkened a vast valley full of Evil Necrotic Trees, and at its farthest reaches were scorched, blistering earth, the wreckage of wasted trees, thorns and thick vines clawing at the stratosphere. A swirl of night sky-purple and darkest green energy warped around the foe.

Nurgal.

There was a heaviness in Abaven. It flowed through his skin like water over stone. I wished I could read him better, but he had blocked me out. I stared between his knuckles at the destruction Nurgal had already caused. How could he go through with a betrayal like this?

Nurgal stood with his back to us, gazing on the canvas he was about to work, thick with the army of Evil Necrotic Trees he had amassed. He had already sent forth his plague of scorched earth, and it sprawled toward Rós's farm and the nearby town. What was left of the forest around us had been caught up in vines and bramble.

Here it was easy to turn the tree folk against man. Here where they had seen the terror man could cause. They were close to the town. They would understand the most. They who had suffered wildfire, deforestation, and plague. Those Tree Folk who had been attacked, as Nurgal called it, were twisted in their anger, and blinded to man's plight.

What they didn't understand is that they could live in harmony. Why couldn't they see that? If things had been different, I believe Abaven could teach man to replant trees, to make the forest stronger. Instead, he strode to Nurgal and grabbed his wrist.

He turned his hollow gaze on us and reached for the hand that gripped me. If there were words between him and Abaven in Root Tongue, then Abaven made it so I was not privy to them.

Nurgal's thorns, branches, and sinews began wrapping around Abaven, drawing him in.

The Fae guard's face was stricken. "This isn't what we agreed on. I was going to be Lord of all that Lasts, remember?"

Nurgal gripped him tighter with a sickly twisted grin.

"No, stop," Abaven begged.

Nurgal continued to entwine him until the Fae disappeared, encased within the creature's body of tangled vines and thorns.

For all appearances, there was no Abaven. Only Nurgal.

And I.

I, the seed.

I who awed at being part of Nurgal while still gripped so tightly by Abaven. He wasn't letting go. And neither was Nurgal.

As we gazed across the valley, we noticed something. Or someone.

Who was there standing before the army of Necrotic Trees, before Nurgal, and the dawn?

> One little red hen.

WHAT THE CLUCK

Rós never stopped to question how she was going to get past all of those corrupted trees. She promised Little Sky that the earth would not be destroyed. No matter the cost, she must get to Nurgal. She puffed out her chest, took up fresh courage, and shot down the hill with a proud cry.

The Evil Necrotic Trees moved toward the hill. The force of their marching rattled Rós's bones. Each step harsher than the last.

BOOM.

BOOM!

Rós scurried toward the trees, hurrying to meet them. They creaked and groaned as they bent to grab her.

Crack

Their long, gray branches curled like fingers. The little red hen squabbled and zipped past the first, then the second.

Rumble, grumble.

The earth shook with the voices of the Evil Necrotic Trees.

Rós wove between them so quickly that it was all a blur.

Washoo

Zhou, zhou.

Scrape. Scrap.

One tree turned and bellowed at her as she ricocheted off its trunk to skirt the next Evil Necrotic Tree. Sap slung from its mouth like enraged spittle.

ROAR

Rós zipped around trunks,

Skitter, skatter.

Over twisted roots,

Whoosh

Through grasping branches,

Wap-a-cha!

Always avoiding their catch at the last second. Her breath came faster than the galloping of horses.

Evil Necrotic Tree roots ripped and snapped from the dry earth. They turned to gather around one of their own that had planted itself to block Rós. One closed in on the other, then another, trying to form a barrier. They crashed together like Titans.

SMASH

The little red hen cackled as she realized she was faster than they. Hope bubbled in her. She could do this!

The line of Evil Necrotic Trees wrapped their branches behind one another, squelching out the sun. Darkness swelled around them. Lightning illuminated a tiny crack between the trunks. This was Rós's chance. She had to take it.

She gave me courage.

If a chicken could face the most powerful forces on earth, so could I. Abaven whispered to me to do the one thing I had been forbidden to do, the thing I wanted and feared most. *Grow.*

The second he let go, I pushed out with ferocity. Roots shot from me, bursting through Nurgal and wrapping around him so tight, they severed his arm. He caterwauled.

Before he could react, there was Rós, pulling me out. I reined myself in enough to escape with her.

You are sunshine in the darkness, I told her.

"Only because you are the sun."

We don't have time to be sentimental. Run!

She squabbled and took off, and Nurgal was after us at once. Evil Necrotic Trees advanced on the town. The earth thundered. I wrapped myself around the hen as lightning snapped from the vortex.

Don't look back!

Of course she looked back. Who doesn't? I slipped to the front of her. *Why did you look back?*

She squawked and zigzagged. *The sky is falling.*

I glanced to the looming vortex. The real sky was corn-moon blue and fiercely stormy. Wind whipped us back. The world had never been darker. And I realized…

A PIECE OF SKY

The sky! In her unfailing faith, her belief in my potential, Rós had made me the sky.

Then I saw Nurgal closing in on us.

Rós, I need you to do something.

Anything!

I need you to eat me.

What? I can't do that.

You must.

Having seen what I could do to Nurgal, knowing what I was capable of, I formed a plan. *What would you do to protect our world, Rós? Would you give yourself for it as I would?*

Before she answered, Nurgal leapt upon us. He caught Rós. She scratched and bit and pecked frantically. He tried to rip me from her, but she was quick and held on tight with her beak.

So there I was, being pulled between good and evil, and I begged Rós, *Eat me! Now!*

I wasn't sure what would happen to me,

but I knew I must not fall into Nurgal's hands. I believed the good in Rós would withstand what I was planning to do.

I can't! Rós cried.

Nurgal tugged, but, miraculously, Rós tugged harder. She gave everything she had. And, unexpectedly, I popped from Nurgal's fingers… right down Rós's throat.

She kind of choked for a moment.

Rós struggled to process the awkward lump in her throat. She opened and closed her mouth, as though doing so would loosen things up. Nurgal stared at her. She gulped.

"No," he growled.

Rós blinked at him. *What happened?*

Nurgal got to his feet. "No."

Rós had the overwhelming sensation that she should probably run. A force rose in her, erupting from her beak in a raucous baw-gawk. She spun and took off. *The sky. I just ate the sky.*

Something within her told her she might die from it.

She glanced behind. Nurgal lunged forward, sweeping his arm across, but missed her, tumbling once again. She zigged and zagged, squawking. For a moment she thought she lost him, but he rose again and stomped forward.

Rós shuddered inside and believed she might be sick. Her stomach swelled. Something worked within her that grew bigger… and BIGGER. Like humongous spiders scuttling through her belly. Pressure mounted, as though she needed to lay the biggest egg in the history of the world *ever*. She skidded to a halt from the pain.

Little Sky, I don't know what to do. I think I'm going to explode!

Nurgal loomed over her. The air that rattled between his vines waxed hot and thick. His hand punched forward, gripping Rós by the neck. He lifted her over his face. *"What have you done?"* he bellowed.

Rós swung from the force of his words, convinced it was the end of the world. For good, this time. She trembled and squeezed her eyes shut tight. The pressure inside was too much. Her legs curled against her belly, claws clenched. She pushed against the agony. A drip of white squirted from her bottom and splattered on Nurgal. Relief instantly swept over her.

He uttered in displeasure. The sound of sizzling followed. He groaned initially, but it grew louder until he roared.

Rós opened one eye. When she realized what it had done to Nurgal, that it was burning into him, a thought struck her. Something inside her urged, *Quick, do more!*

So she did.

    Like… a lot.

        All over the place.

An unnatural noise surged from Nurgal. A scream of terrible pain. Steam hissed from him. The vines and bramble that twisted to form him began to fall apart and shrivel. The green withered away from his face, revealing fair skin underneath. A shock of silver hair lay across the brow.

Rós fell to the ground in a heap as Nurgal lost control of his grip. He grabbed his seared face, ripping at it. He swung and writhed. "No. NO!"

The rest of his body peeled away, revealing more and more of the captive inside. Nurgal slipped away in a puddle of liquified green, seeping into the earth. There stood Abaven against the dawn. The Evil Necrotic Trees froze, leaderless.

Abaven stooped to Rós and smiled. "You did it."

Rós blinked. *What just happened?*

"I could not tell you before, little one. I thought often on the seed during my imprisonment on the mountain. I knew it would be safe with the Fae. However, since Nurgal had stolen it, the world lay in peril."

He took a deep breath and continued. "I believed that if I planted it in Nurgal, instead of allowing him to plant it, it would weaken him. Though I remained unsure if it would be enough to defeat him. There was one thing I had not counted on."

He gazed steadily at the little red hen, a slow smile tilting the corner of his mouth. "You."

The Fae guardian chuckled. "By some stroke of providence, you came along. You showed the seed the goodness in the world. You showed what the world could be, what the seed could be, and that is what it chose. And the goodness in you magnified it, so that when both parts of you combined touched Nurgal, he was destroyed."

What. The. Cluck.

"Forgive me for being so secretive. I had to play my part. Allow me to make it right." Abaven stretched out his arms to her.

The little red hen turned her head from one side, then to the other. Could she really trust him? He had tricked her once.

The brown around him receded, leaving only a thick halo of purple. Even the wall of white diminished. Something inside her told her to trust him. Something about having a little piece of sky in all of us.

CHICKEN LITTLE

Abaven set Rós down at the edge of the farm. They stood together by The Mare's pasture. She raised her gray head with a swish of her tail. Her ears flicked.

Abaven smiled at her. The Mare whickered and cantered to him, dropping her head against his hand. He spoke in a strange language Rós did not understand. The Mare seemed to understand him, however, and bobbed her head, nudging him back. She ambled off to her high hill overlooking the farm.

What did you say to her? Rós asked.

Abaven kept his eyes fixed on The

A PIECE OF SKY

Mare. "Only to continue to send brave souls out into the world."

Did you know each other?

Abaven gazed down at the little red hen. The calm, gentle smile remained etched upon his face. "Once upon a time."

Rós took a deep breath. *I should probably go.*

He nodded. "What's inside you is beautiful. Never lose that."

The hen nodded and turned. This time she didn't look back.

Rós stood on the edge of Farmer's yard. Dog was not present, and she wondered if he wasn't out in the highlands with Farmer and the sheep.

From all appearances, nothing had changed while she was away.

She made her way to the coop to take up a spot in her old nest. Grania dozed beside her. Though they had quarreled, Rós welcomed the swelling in her heart to see her friend safe and well. She nestled down, grinding her beak contentedly.

Thinking about the danger she faced, how close the war came to the farm and to destroying man, made her realize life would never be the same again.

In fact, sitting here seemed completely boring. A whisper within her said she was meant for more.

She leaned over to Grania and bawked softly.

Grania's eyes opened. "Rós?" She jumped straight up from her nest. "Rós!"

Rós smiled up at her. "Hello," she said.

"You're alive!"

"Of course I'm alive. I have the sky in me."

"I don't understand."

Rós preened herself nonchalantly. "I was right. The piece of sky turned out to be something really big, and I was the one who could stop it. Did we agree on five eggs?"

Grania sank into her nest, beak agape.

Rós chortled. "Might want to get started on that."

"How big was it?" Grania asked slowly.

"Oh, you know… the end of the world."

Grania gaped at her. "The end of the—you saved the world?"

Rós tucked her head under her wing and sighed, missing the golden piece of sky.

"If I didn't know it happened, then no one will ever know it happened."

"That's alright." Rós shrugged.

"It's not alright, they owe their lives to us. You saved the world, Rós. Such a big thing for a small chicken."

The little red hen raised her head and looked plainly at her friend.

"No one is too small to change the world."

And you never knew it happened. But you do now. Because, like Little Sky, you have divine purpose and will. Embrace it. There's a piece of sky in all of us, and now the responsibility is on your shoulders to tell everyone that no soul is too small to change the world.

Be the acorn...

Who chose to be the sky.

About the Author

Multi-award winning author, Ann Hunter, is the creator of the young adult fantasy series Crowns of the Twelve (including the novels *The Subtle Beauty, Moonlight, Fallen,* and *A Piece of Sky,* with *Ashes* and *The Rose In The Briar* to follow).

She likes cherry soda with chocolate ice cream, is a mom first and a writer second, has a secret identity, and thinks the Twilight movies are cheesier than cheez whiz (which is why they are her guilty pleasure!)

She lives in a cozy Utah home with her two awesome kids and epic husband.

Thank you for reading *A Piece of Sky*
Please leave a review on Amazon and Goodreads.
Your opinion matters! Even if it is only 1-2 sentences.
Amazon: http://amzn.com/B00PI4BNZY

Ann would love to connect with you!
If you would like to hear about upcoming novels
and reviews, please check out her author page:
https://www.facebook.com/authorannhunter

You can get a sneak peek at works in progress at
http://wattpad.com/AnnHunter82

Baw-gawk!

Made in the USA
San Bernardino, CA
05 September 2015